simon and schuster
First published in Great Britain in 2014 by Simon and Schuster UK Ltd
1st Floor, 222 Gray's Inn Road, London WC1X 8HB
A CBS Company
Publication Licensed by Mercis Publishing bv, Amsterdam

ISBN 978-1-4711-2147-0
Printed and bound in China
10 9 8 7 6 5 4 3 2 1
www.simonandschuster.co.uk
www.miffy.com

miffy's play date

SIMON AND SCHUSTER
London New York Sydney Toronto New Delhi

Miffy is looking out of the window.
She is waiting for her friend, Grunty.

Today, they have a play date!

Miffy can't wait to show Grunty
all of her toys.

Find these stickers and add them to the picture:

Knock Knock!

Grunty is here!

Miffy and Grunty are very happy to see each other.

Find these stickers and add them to the picture:

Here are some of Miffy's toys.

'Shall we play with blocks, Grunty?'
Miffy asks.
'Let's make a castle!' Grunty says.

That looks very nice.

'What shall we do now?'

Find these stickers and add them to the picture:

Miffy gets the paper, scissors and some pencils too.
Miffy draws a shape and Grunty cuts it out.

Look – bunny ears!

Find these stickers and add them to the picture:

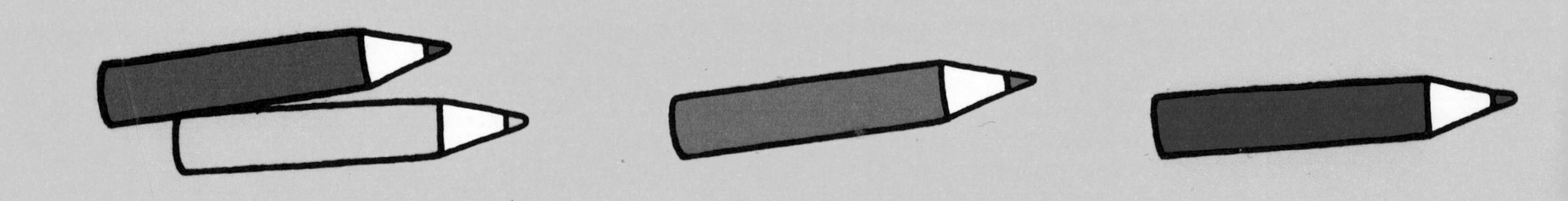

Grunty is wearing her new ears. This is so much fun!

Next, the friends decide to play hide and seek. Miffy counts while Grunty finds a place to hide.

Find these stickers and add them to the picture:

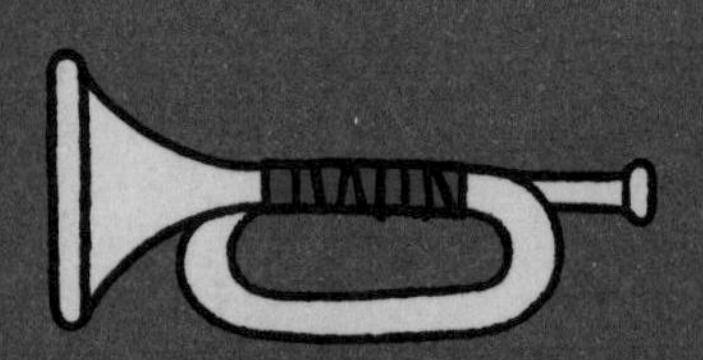

'Ready or not, here I come!'

Miffy looks everywhere until she hears a giggle coming from inside the play tent.

'Got you!' Miffy cries.

Find these stickers and add them to the picture:

Now for a quiet game.
Miffy and Grunty are pretending to go shopping.

'Let's go to the pretend toy shop,' says Miffy.
'I would like to buy a pretend kite,' says Grunty.

Find these stickers and add them to the picture:

Playing makes Miffy and Grunty hungry.

Mmm. The grapes taste sweet.

Now they are ready to play again!

Find these stickers and add them to the picture:

Soon it is time to clean up the toys.

Miffy puts her train away and Grunty helps pick up the toys from playing pretend toy shopping.

Find these stickers and add them to the picture:

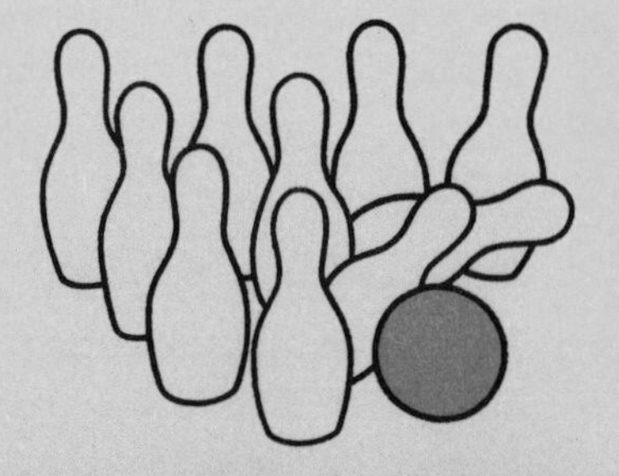

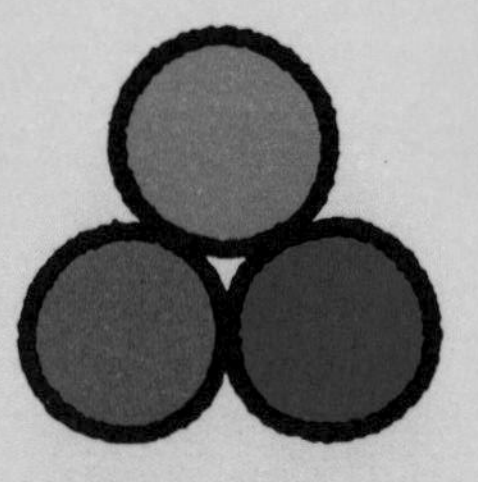

Knock Knock!
It's time for Grunty to go home.

Grunty looks sad.
Miffy and Grunty don't want their play date to end.

Find these stickers and add them to the picture:

Miffy gives Grunty the paper bunny ears to take home.

'Thank you, Miffy,' says Grunty.
'You're welcome, Grunty,'
says Miffy.

Find these stickers and add them to the picture:

Mummy Bunny and Miffy wave goodbye to Grunty through the window.

What a fun play date!

Bye-bye!

Find these stickers and add them to the picture: